The Mailbo

Treasure
FROM LAKE TITICACA

Written by GS McClellan

For more information please visit the website:
www.TheMailboxAdventures.com

Contents

1

The Attic

The room smelled like mustard, sharp cheddar cheese and dust. It was Joey's nightly snack (the mustard and sharp cheddar, not the dust), which he folded into one piece of white bread. He savored each bite as he joined his sister Josie, who was exploring the musty, cluttered attic of their old Vermont farmhouse.

"Whoa, look what I found," Joey said, swallowing the last piece of sandwich whole. He held a large gray object in his hands.

"An old mailbox?" Josie asked.

Joey nodded slowly with pleasure as he inspected the mailbox from every angle. Joey was a kid who didn't watch much TV. Playing on the computer wasn't his thing, either. But he loved to collect things. Joey had a collection of license plates that covered a whole wall of his room. In a big metal container on his desk sat more than a thousand bottle caps he had collected on his walks to and from school. His windowsills were lined from end to end with one of every Star Wars action figured ever made, and his University of Vermont garbage pail had been converted to a storage facility for his expanding collection of yellow rubber ducks. But for now, he wasn't concerned with any of those things. His attention was focused squarely on the old mailbox, which he thought might be the start of another great collection.

"Is this our old mailbox?" Joey asked Josie, as his finger made one last sweep across his back molars, harvesting every last bit of mustard and cheese he could.

"We've never had a mailbox like *that*," she said dismissively.

Joey knew that their old Vermont farmhouse had been around since the early 1700s. But his family had only lived in it since the year 2000, so there was no telling whose mailbox it could have been. He dusted it off with his shirt and carried it down the attic steps to his bedroom on the third floor.

Joey knew his mom wouldn't want him keeping an old, grimy mailbox in his room. She was trying to get him to take stuff *out* of his room, not add new things to it. But the idea of an old mailbox collection excited Joey. He plunked it on his desk next to the canister of bottle caps.

Just then, his dad called up the stairs from the hallway below. "Time for bed." Joey relayed the message to his sister who was still in the attic exploring.

"Aww, but I don't want to go to bed," she protested, stomping down the stairs.

Joey, on the other hand, liked bedtime. He didn't like homework time and he didn't like bath time. But he liked bedtime, especially on weekend nights when his mom and dad allowed him to sleep in the teepee he built in his room.

Joey brushed his teeth quickly, as always; just enough to make his mouth smell like toothpaste so his parents wouldn't make him brush them again. He changed into his pajamas, hollered "goodnight" from the top of the stairs and climbed into the pile of blankets in his teepee. The cone shaped crooked structure that Joey had built with long sticks and twin sized sheets was truly his own private space, something his dad said everyone should have. No one, not even the dog, a Newfoundland named Michigan, was allowed in. But this particular weekend night would be different than any other Joey had spent in his teepee.

2

The Mailbox

Joey was awoken by an unusually bright light beaming through the walls of the teepee. He rubbed his tired eyes as he poked his head out from under the blankets. His first thought was that his dad was coming to check on him with a flashlight, but the light wasn't moving like a flashlight would. In fact, it wasn't moving at all. Joey picked up a toy robot that was stashed under one of the blankets and peeked its head out of the teepee. Still the light didn't move. *What could it be?* Joey wondered. He peeked his own head out for a look. The light was much brighter than it first appeared to him through the teepee wall. He shaded his eyes, which were still waking up from the darkness of sleep. Slowly, he got used to the bright, golden glow and saw that it was coming from the mailbox.

Curious, Joey crawled out of his teepee and made his way toward the glowing mailbox. He passed the alarm clock on the floor near his bed. It was 12:24am. When he got close enough, Joey held his hand over the top of the mailbox to see if it was hot. It was not. He didn't hear any unusual sounds or smell any unusual odors either.

Joey poked the mailbox with a shoe he found under his desk. Nothing. There was only one thing left for Joey to do: open it. He crawled under his bed to retrieve the back scratcher he had gotten for Christmas: the kind with a small hand on the end of it. Sitting as far away as he could, he leaned toward the mailbox and hooked the backscratcher into the handle on the mailbox door. He closed his eyes and pulled.

Creaaak. The door swung open slowly.

He opened his eyes.

Bright golden rays of light poured out from the inside of the mailbox, filling his room. His heart started pounding even faster than before. Joey peered inside and saw a letter. He reached in, clasped onto the letter with his thumb and index finger, and slowly pulled it out of the mailbox. The mailbox stopped glowing, and a soft blue light started to emerge from the envelope. Joey could hardly believe his eyes. He remembered checking inside the mailbox before bringing it to his room: it had definitely been empty. And he absolutely, positively knew that the mailbox was not glowing when he found it in the attic. He sat on the floor of his room, holding the letter. A single beam of faded blue light rose up from the letter toward the ceiling. Joey read the front of the envelope:

To: Joey Jimmer-Jefferson

Farmhouse in the Woods

Vermont

He was thunderstruck when he saw his name on the envelope. He could feel the hair on the back of his neck stand up. The way it was addressed was curious, to say the least. Usually people sent letters to his street address. He looked next at the upper left corner of the envelope to see who it was from.

From: Gustavo Quispe

Joey didn't recognize the name. He started to open the envelope, but then stopped himself. He was eager and timid all at once. He felt the way he did earlier that day, when his basketball coach asked him if he wanted to go into the game. The week before, Joey had made a bad pass, which the other team intercepted and ran down the court for the game winning shot. *I might make a mistake. I might throw an air ball or a bad pass and lose the game for my team,* he remembered thinking to himself as his coach waited for his decision. He wanted to go in the game, but he also didn't. He felt the same way about the letter. He wanted to open it, but he also didn't. He was afraid of what might happen.

He looked up from the envelope. Through the faded blue light he could see the evergreen trees in his backyard, which swayed and creaked in the evening breeze. Then, in the same blue glow, he saw on the edge of his desk the book he was reading for school. It was a book about Theodore Roosevelt, whose courage Joey admired greatly. *What would he do?* Joey asked himself. It didn't take long for the answer to come.

3

The Letter

Joey slid his fingers gently underneath the flap on the back of the envelope, took a deep breath, and opened it. The letter inside was written on thick paper with black ink. Joey didn't understand any of the words, as they appeared to be written in a language he had never seen. But as he held the letter, something amazing began to happen: the letters started moving on the paper. They changed shape and size. Then they began scrambling around the page like bugs scattering in the light. Joey watched with amazement as the words began to translate themselves into English. In a matter of moments, Joey was able to read the letter.

> Dear Mailbox,
>
> I am in danger. Please find someone with courage to help me.
>
> Sincerely,
>
> Gustavo Quispe

A thousand questions were now spinning through Joey's head. Why would someone write to a mailbox? Usually people wrote to a person, not a mailbox. And how did this person, Gustavo Quispe, send a letter through the old mailbox? Joey wondered for a moment if his sister could be playing a trick on him. But there was no way she could make the mailbox glow, or the envelope shine blue, or the words change shape on the piece of paper.

As Joey sat in his room trying to figure it all out, he began to wonder if the mailbox he had found was magic. This possibility was almost too much for Joey to believe. But he knew one thing: the teepee was the best place for him to think this mystery through.

He put the letter back into the mailbox for safe keeping before turning back toward his teepee. But as soon as he put the letter back into the mailbox, an enormous ray of the same blue light shot out and wrapped around Joey, lifting him off the ground. With a loud swoosh of air, like a train passing by a station platform at high speed, the mailbox sucked it all back in: the letter, the blue light, and Joey.

4

Gustavo Quispe

It happened very fast. One second Joey was in his room, the next he was in someone else's room. To say Joey was scared wouldn't be quite accurate. Terrified would be a better word. He could feel his hands shaking as he anxiously scanned the new surroundings for clues. His posters, his desk, his teepee, were all gone. He turned his head the other way looking for his backpack, but it was nowhere to be seen either. Instead, he saw walls made of brown bricks. There was a flag with red, yellow and green stripes hanging from the ceiling and a narrow bookshelf standing next to the door. He was sitting on the floor, which was covered with a thin, brightly colored rug, and there was a bed against the wall between two small windows. Through the windows Joey saw a sapphire blue lake glistening in the sunlight, with snow-capped mountains in the distance. He felt the cool breeze of the lake air on his skin, as it blew through the window, and watched as a large bird with white, black and grey feathers flew past.

"Kamisaraki!"

Joey jumped nearly six inches off the floor. He turned his head toward the voice and saw a young boy standing behind him. The boy looked to be about the same age as Joey, 9 years old. Joey sprang to his feet and looked intently at the boy, who was wearing a green t-shirt and grey pants tied at the waist. His hair was jet black and his skin was a shiny, deep brown.

"I am Gustavo Quispe," the boy said slowly.

Joey's stomach jumped. Gustavo Quispe was the name on the letter in the mailbox!

"Ummm....My name is Joey Jimmer-Jefferson."

"*Winus tiyas.*"

Joey did not understand. "Do you speak English?"

"*Jisa.*" Gustavo said with a smile. "Yes. A little bit."

Then Gustavo repeated what he had said to Joey in his native language of Aymara, only this time adding the English.

"*Kamisaraki...*Hello. *Winus tiyas...*Good morning."

Joey didn't know where to begin. He wanted to know where he was, and how he got there. Was Gustavo the same Gustavo who sent the letter? But before he could ask any of his questions, Gustavo asked *him* a question.

"Can you help me?"

5

The Headdress

Joey was frozen with fear. He just stood and stared at Gustavo, second-guessing his decision to open the letter.

Gustavo reached into his closet and pulled out a shiny piece of gold that was about twice the size of his hand. It had a strange looking face on the front.

"What is *that*?" Joey asked sheepishly.

"A headdress."

"A headdress?" Joey repeated. He had never heard of such a thing.

Gustavo explained that his father, an archaeologist, found the headdress, which would have been worn by someone during special ceremonies.

This was getting interesting. Joey could feel some of his fear beginning to go away. "Where did he find it? What ceremonies?" Joey asked, as he reached out to touch the gleaming piece of gold.

Gustavo explained in the best English he could that his father had found the headdress on the Isla Del Sol, which was an

island in the lake he could see from the window of his room.

Joey looked out at the island, which looked like a long narrow

strip of brown and green rock surrounded by glistening rich

blue water. Joey listened as Gustavo explained that while no

one really knows exactly how the headdress was used, most

think it may have been worn for a wedding, or to show that the person wearing it was important. Or maybe, Gustavo explained, it was used to scare invaders away from the island.

"How old is it?"

"My *auqui*...um, my father, thinks it might be 2,000 years old."

"Whoa," Joey said. "That's old! Why do you have it in your closet?"

"I...I am hiding it." Gustavo stammered.

"Hiding it?" Joey asked in a surprised tone of voice. "Why?"

Gustavo gazed down at the ground and took a deep breath. "The day my father found it was also the day he got sick."

"Sick?"

"Yes. Some people say the headdress is cursed, which is why he got sick. But I don't believe that, because I have had it in my room for the last two days and I am not sick."

Joey nodded his head in agreement. Gustavo's reasoning made sense to Joey. "Is your dad okay?"

"I don't know," Gustavo said slowly. "He's been at the hospital in La Paz for the last two days. They said he was dehydrated."

Joey wasn't sure where La Paz was, but he figured it was the closest city with a hospital. "Is your mom with him?" Joey asked.

Gustavo turned his head away and wiped his eyes. Joey could tell Gustavo was about to cry. "She died last year," Gustavo said softly.

Joey felt a pit in his stomach. He was sorry he asked the question. But even more, he couldn't imagine what it would be like for his own mother to die.

Gustavo turned his head back toward Joey, wanting to change the topic. "I hid the headdress in my closet to keep it safe until he comes back."

"That was a good idea," Joey said, still trying to get over what it must be like for Gustavo to have lost his mother, and be alone in his house while his dad was in the hospital. Joey was beginning to realize that he had never known fear like Gustavo had known fear. His basketball games began to seem pretty small in comparison.

"But it can't stay here anymore," Gustavo said quickly.

"It can't?"

"The newspaper wrote about it this week. Now that people know my father is the one who found it, treasure hunters will come looking for it. It needs to go to the museum."

"Treasure hunters?" Joey asked.

"Yes...treasure hunters, like the ones who stole gold from the tombs of Egyptian Pharaohs. Treasure hunters have been trying to find this headdress for years. Now that they know it has been found, they will want to steal it."

"Oh," Joey said cautiously. This was beginning to sound scary. "So....why do you need *my* help?"

"I need you to take it to the museum."

"What?"

"No one will know you have it. You can get it safely there."

"Why can't you just call the museum and ask them to come get it?" Joey asked.

"It's been closed for the last two days. They open later today, but I'm afraid the treasure hunters will get here before then."

"Why can't you just give it to a neighbor?" Joey protested, trying to find any way out of needing to be the one to take this headdress to the museum.

"Some of the neighbors think it is cursed and won't come near it. Others don't want it because they know the treasure hunters will come after them. You are my only hope."

"But I don't know where the museum is."

"I made you a map," Gustavo said.

Joey took a deep breath. "Is this why you sent me the letter? Actually, how *did* you send that letter to me, anyway?"

6

Gustavo's Mailbox

Gustavo pointed to his closet and motioned for Joey to look inside. Joey took a few steps toward the closet and peeked his head in.

"What do you see?" Gustavo asked.

"A messy closet?" Joey said.

"No, no," Gustavo said, directing Joey with a wave of his hand to look in the corner of his closet.

Now Joey saw it: A rectangular box covered in chipping blue paint leaning against the wall. "What is that?" Joey asked.

"A mailbox."

Chills ran down Joey's back. *A mailbox?* He felt excited, as if he was on the verge of a discovery. But he didn't know why.

"I found it in the street last year." Gustavo said. "Someone threw it out. Where did you find your mailbox?"

"In my attic," Joey said slowly, wondering how Gustavo knew about his mailbox. "Does yours look like mine?" Gustavo asked.

"No," Joey said. "Mine looks like a bird house with a red roof. How did you know I found a mailbox?"

"It's how you got here. You opened my letter and it brought you to my room. Mine works the same way."

Joey looked in amazement at Gustavo and then again at his old, blue mailbox. "How does it work?"

"It's magic."

"Magic? What do you mean?"

"When you opened the letter, it translated itself into your language, right?"

Joey nodded in agreement.

"Then when you put the open letter back into the mailbox," Gustavo explained, "you were telling the mailbox that you agree to help. So, it sucked you into the mailbox and brought you here. Every mailbox adventure begins the same way."

Joey looked out Gustavo's window in silence. So many questions raced through his head.

"Does any mailbox work?" Joey asked, turning his eyes away from the lake back toward Gustavo.

"I think it's only mailboxes that people have stopped using," Gustavo explained, "at least that's what the others say."

"Others?"

"*Jisa*...Um, yes. I have received three letters from other people."

"What?" Joey couldn't believe his ears. "From where?"

"France, Australia, and North Dakota."

"And did the mailbox take you to all those places?"

"Yes."

Joey was speechless. Gustavo stood calmly as Joey let it all sink in.

"So how did your letter come to me?"

"The letter I wrote said I needed someone who was courageous. The mailbox found you."

Joey gulped hard. "So you didn't know I had a mailbox?"

"Nope. I just wrote my letter and put it in the mailbox. The mailbox found you. That's why the writing on the envelope wasn't the same as the writing on the letter. Did you notice that?"

Joey thought back to the letter he opened in his room, and remembered that the address on the envelope was definitely written in a different style than Gustavo's letter. In fact, the address seemed burned onto the envelope.

"So, where are we right now?" Joey realized that in all the excitement and confusion he had never asked where Gustavo lived.

"Bolivia."

"Bolivia?" Joey blurted. He thought about the poster in his room of the seven continents. He knew he'd seen Bolivia on the map, but he couldn't place where it was. Then he remembered.

"South America?" Joey announced in a voice of disbelief.

"*Jisa*," Gustavo said with a smile.

Joey couldn't seem to stop shaking his head. He was filled with disbelief and amazement. This was all very sudden and hard to believe. His mother always told him that magic was only real in movies. But this mailbox adventure was one hundred percent real *and* one hundred percent magic.

7

Salteñas

"How about some breakfast before we get started?" Gustavo asked.

Joey's eyes lit up. He realized he was hungry too. Gustavo led the way out of his room and into the hallway toward the kitchen. He pulled a few boxes off of the shelves and began to mix some flour in a bowl. Joey didn't do much cooking at his home, but watching Gustavo work made him wish he knew more about it.

"What are you making?" Joey asked.

"Salteñas."

Joey had no idea what that meant, but he was hungry, and he knew he would probably eat just about anything Gustavo served him.

As they waited for the food to cook in the oven, Gustavo told Joey about his village, and how he learned to cook for his father after his mother died. Gustavo also told Joey about how his dad had secretly sent the headdress to him when he fell sick, convincing a co-worker that the quickly wrapped package was instructions for his son while he was away in the hospital. Joey listened intently before telling Gustavo about his dog Michigan, his sister Josie, and his many collections. But what he really wanted to know more about was the headdress. Gustavo explained that it was solid gold, which was extremely valuable. But more than that, it was something that people have been trying to find for many years. His father never wanted to find it because he knew it would bring trouble from thieves. But he always told Gustavo that if he ever did find it during one of his archaeological expeditions, he would take it straight to the museum.

"He always told me to do the same thing. 'If you ever find it and I am not with you, make sure you take it to the museum immediately.' That's why he made sure it got to me. That's why it needs to go to the museum today."

"So the people he worked with knew he found it, but now they don't know where it has gone?"

"Yes, that is correct." Gustavo confirmed. "And once the paper wrote the story, everyone knew about it."

From Gustavo's description, Joey could tell that the headdress was more valuable (and more dangerous) than anything he had ever known. He was beginning to think he wanted to help Gustavo if he could, he just wasn't really sure he knew how.

But his thoughts quickly changed to food, as the smell of the cooking salteñas began wafting through the kitchen. When Gustavo took them out of the oven, they looked like the strombolis Joey liked to order at his favorite pizza place in Vermont. Joey could barely contain his hunger. He took a big bite. It was hot and spicy. He could taste potatoes and onions and hard-boiled eggs. He could tell there were raisins in there as well, which he would normally never eat. But today, they tasted better than any raisin he had ever had.

8

Treasure Hunters

Joey was just finishing his second salteña when a loud pounding sound vibrated the front door.

Gustavo grabbed Joey's arm and pulled him away from the table into the hallway. He peeked out to the street from the side window and saw two men standing at the front door. They were banging on the door with a large rock. Gustavo ran to his room to get the headdress. Joey followed, his heart starting to pound fast again. Gustavo opened Joey's hand and put the headdress in it. Then he reached into his pocket and pulled out a folded piece of paper, which he also put in Joey's hand.

"This is the map to the museum. Please help me."

Boom...Boom. The banging on the door got louder. Gustavo brought Joey through the house to the back door and opened it.

"Go. Please."

BOOM! Joey heard another loud bang that sounded like it was going to break the door down. Gustavo looked at Joey with desperation. Joey was afraid. But somehow the mailbox

had chosen him for his courage. Maybe Theodore Roosevelt was right when he said everybody has the potential to be courageous. Maybe. Joey took a deep breath, clenched his fingers tight around the headdress and map, and ran out the back door into the street.

*****

Joey was only a few steps away when he heard some commotion in the house. He tiptoed back and peeked through the window. He could see that Gustavo had opened the front door and the men were searching the house. One was tall and skinny with a bald head, the other was short and fat. Joey watched as the men opened drawers and pulled books off shelves. After a few minutes of searching, Joey saw the taller man begin to holler at Gustavo. Joey gulped as he saw sprays of spit, lots of it, spew from the angry man's lips. Joey couldn't quite tell, but he thought the man was yelling in Spanish. The men huffed through the hallway toward the front door. As they opened it, Joey knew it was time to go. He turned and ran away from the house.

9

The Chase

Joey stopped at a street sign to catch his breath and open the map that Gustavo had given him. It had a picture of a giant blue lake on it, with the words "Lake Titicaca" written over it.

That must be the lake he saw from Gustavo's house, Joey thought to himself.

The words at the top of the map were underlined with a bright green marker: "Copacabana, Bolivia."

He looked closer at the map and saw a bright red circle around the words: "Museo del Poncho." He guessed that was where he needed to go. But how would he get there? He looked up at the street sign.

Av 6 de Agosto

Joey searched the map. He was only one street away!

Joey began to fold the map back up when he heard someone yell from across the street.

Joey looked up and saw two men pointing at him, the same men who had searched Gustavo's house. He glanced down and realized what they were pointing at: he was still carrying the gold headdress in his hand. In his haste to leave he hadn't thought to hide it. The men took off running across the street in pursuit of Joey.

Joey started running too, but the *Av 6 de Agosto* was crowded with people, making it hard for Joey to run as fast as he wanted to. He passed by a street vendor selling hats stacked high in piles. Next to her, another woman sat on the sidewalk selling round loaves of bread from a blanket. Joey could smell freshly cooked corn and the sweet aroma of fried dough. Joey loved fried dough, it reminded him of the circus. But there was no time to think about the circus now. Joey needed to get away from the chasing thieves.

He decided to turn down a small side-street called Bolivar. It was the only chance he had of escaping the men. Joey could feel his heart pounding high in his throat.

"Oh, man," Joey sighed. He stopped running. Bolivar Street was packed with people. It was much more crowded than *Av 6 de Agosto*. He thought about turning around, but he looked back and realized that the men had already turned down Bolivar after him. He had no choice but to keep going.

People were everywhere on Bolivar Street: most seemed to be spilling out into the street from the park that ran alongside. It was a big park, but not big enough for the thousands of people there that day. As Joey began to weave his way through the throngs of people, his arm got caught on a person's bag. The headdress came loose in his hands, which he juggled a few times before regaining control. But he wasn't able to hold onto the map, which fell out of his hand and floated to the street below. Frantically, Joey started searching for the map, but with so many people on the street it was hard to see where it had gone. He looked back and saw that the two treasure hunters were closing in on him, but he absolutely had to find the map or he would have no chance of saving the headdress. He fell to his knees and started crawling on the street, desperately hunting for the piece of paper. Time was running out. He turned his head back toward the direction of the two men, whose faces he could see clearly now.

And then he saw it. The map was stuck to the foot of an old gray donkey who was being led through the streets by his elderly owner. Joey jumped to his feet and ran toward the donkey, knowing with every bone in his body that running toward the animal was not a good idea, because it meant he was also running toward the thieves. But he had no choice.

The thieves saw him running closer and picked up their pace, confident they were about to get the headdress. Joey made it to the donkey first and dove for the piece of paper stuck to the right rear hoof. Startled by the commotion, the donkey reared back on his hind legs and bicycle kicked his front legs in the air. The elderly owner jerked the reins to calm his donkey down, as the two men in pursuit of Joey jumped back from the donkey, whose angrily kicking front legs had come close to connecting with their faces. Joey scrambled to his feet, feeling no pain from diving on the street, and began running in the opposite direction. The donkey was still upset, which was preventing the thieves from getting by on the crowded street. Joey ran as fast as he possibly could, knowing that he had very narrowly escaped disaster.

10

The Parade

Joey was almost completely out of breath. He remembered how his coach had made his team run the length of the court during basketball practice. But this felt like he had run the length of fifty courts. Huffing deep gasps of air, he made a quick glance behind him to look for the thieves, who were still trying to get past the commotion of the flustered donkey. But as Joey was looking in that direction, a man on stilts wearing a giant peacock costume walked in front of him.

"*What the...*" Joey thought to himself.

Then another person, wearing bright pink feathers on her arms, brushed past Joey.

Joey turned to look at the back of her feathers, which seemed to have giant black and white eyes sewn on to them. Instead, he saw a man in a long cape walking toward him, with red, yellow and green lines painted on his face. Another man in a giant fish suit ran between them, almost knocking Joey over.

Joey spun around, avoiding the man in the fish costume. That's when he saw the floats. These were the same kind of

floats he had seen in the Rose Bowl Parade on TV, only much bigger. One was a giant bird with flapping wings. There was also a mermaid float. But the biggest and most amazing of all was the dragon float. The dragon was bright red and green. Its head, which seemed as large as Joey's house in Vermont, was covered with glitter that sparkled in the sunlight. Joey made his way through the crowd to get a closer look. When he got to the float, he noticed an opening under the tail. He ducked his head and went in. At least he could get a few minutes to catch his breath without being seen by the thieves.

It was dark underneath the float. There were rows of rubber wheels on both sides, and long wooden planks above. Joey sat down and rested for a minute, still fairly confident that the men wouldn't find him there. But then the wheels started moving. Joey jumped up and realized that there was almost enough room for him to stand straight up. He walked along under the float as it moved across the grass of the park. Then he felt the float go over the bump of a curb and the wheels bounce on the pavement of the road. He could hear people cheering. He peeked outside the opening and saw that the street was packed with people. Dancers ran up alongside the float and spun each other around. The crowd roared.

As the float made its way along the parade route, Joey realized he had no idea where it was going. If he got too far away, he knew he would never find the museum.

Joey decided to run. He ducked his head and scurried out from the opening behind the giant dragon. Weaving his way through the dancers, he made it to the sidewalk. He looked around for a street sign to try to figure out where he was.

The first sign he saw told him he was on *Jauregui* Street. He looked at his map and saw that he had gone one street past the museum. He didn't have far to go.

He quickly glanced over his shoulder to see if the men were still following him....but seeing nothing, he started running through the crowd. He bumped into people as he tried to make his way through, but most people didn't seem to notice.

Then, suddenly, somebody grabbed his arm. The nerves in Joey's stomach went wild.

"*Kamisaraki*, Joey Jimmer-Jefferson."

11

The Poncho

Joey turned violently to wrestle himself free from the person's grip, thinking he had been caught. But as he turned, he saw Gustavo's face.

"Oh man…" Joey sighed in relief. "What are you doing here? You almost scared me to death."

"Don't worry. I heard the men shout after they left my house. I saw them start to chase you and thought you might need help, so I followed you. Put this on."

Gustavo had brought Joey a traditional Bolivian poncho, the same type Joey could see many of the men on the street wearing. It was more colorful than any piece of clothing Joey had ever seen. The colors were bright purple, pink and neon green. It was easy to put on. He just put his head through and let it drop down on his shoulders.

"This will help you blend in," Gustavo said.

"Thanks," Joey said, as he adjusted the poncho over his shirt. It was the first time Joey realized that he was still wearing his pajamas.

"What is this parade?" Joey asked, as the nerves in his stomach began to settle.

"Carnaval," Gustavo said.

"Car – nah – vall?" Joey repeated, trying to say it the same way Gustavo did.

"Yes. It's the biggest parade in the world. Lots of countries celebrate Carnaval. Our parade lasts for three days."

"Three days?" Joey said. He knew he had never seen anything like this in Vermont. He wondered if there were any Carnaval parades in America.

Gustavo grasped Joey's hands to get his attention, then looked him straight in the eye. "These men are very dangerous. They will do anything to get the headdress from you. I saw a tattoo on the taller man's arm when they searched my house. I recognized it from something my father showed me. It is the sign of the Quizquiz."

"Quizquiz?" Joey laughed. "That doesn't sound too scary."

"Quizquiz was the last Emperor of the Incan people. Remember the Isla Del Sol, where that headdress was found?" Gustavo asked, pointing to Joey's hand still griped tight around the artifact. "That's where the Incas lived. Those men chasing you believe we stole this headdress from the Incan people."

Joey's smile turned to a frown. "The Quizquiz gang is feared throughout all of South America," Gustavo continued. "As quickly as you can, you need to get the headdress to the museum. Go to *Santivanez* Street, then *Calle Baptista*. The museum will be there. Meet me at the lake when you are finished. You will see it from the museum."

Joey nodded in agreement, as Gustavo disappeared into the crowded street. Joey was scared: more scared now than ever, knowing who he was up against. But at the same time he was focused on helping his new friend. He wanted to be as courageous as the mailbox thought he could be.

As he watched Gustavo walk away, he realized it would be better for him to walk, too. Running would only draw attention to himself. He turned onto *Santivanez* Street, as Gustavo had said. He looked around. The men were nowhere to be seen. He felt his nerves begin to settle. *Maybe I shook them off,* Joey thought to himself. His confidence was beginning to grow. In a few minutes, he saw *Calle Baptista* and turned. He could see the museum ahead.

12

Doubts

"Oh, no," Joey muttered to himself. He stopped in his tracks and began walking backwards. The two thieves were standing at the front door of the museum. How did they know he was headed to the museum? Joey's stomach dropped. Had Gustavo told them? Why would he do that? Was this whole thing a set up to get Joey caught with the artifact? Joey was very nervous now. He had trusted Gustavo from the very beginning, but now he was beginning to doubt. He found a tree around the corner and leaned against it as he tried to put together a plan.

Maybe I should just leave the headdress on the street and run, he thought to himself. But then how would he explain that to Gustavo? Joey still had no idea how to get back to Vermont. For that, he knew he needed Gustavo's help. Leaving the headdress on the street wasn't a good option. *But what then*?

As he stood against the tree in the warm Bolivian sun, he couldn't think of any other way the men could have known that Joey was headed to the museum, other than Gustavo telling them when they searched his house. But then he remembered what Gustavo had said in the kitchen earlier that day, that if the headdress was ever found, his father said it needed to be brought to the museum. Maybe the thieves heard what Gustavo said through the kitchen window? Maybe they were listening before they slammed the rock against the door?

The more he thought about it, the more he realized that Gustavo had no reason to lie to him. But he had to be sure if he was going to continue to help him. He made his way to the lake, without passing the museum.

When he got there, Gustavo was excited to see him. "That was quick. What happened?"

"The treasure hunters are waiting at the museum."

"Oh, no, no, no," Gustavo whined. A look of panic came across his face.

"How do you think the men knew I was going to the museum?"

Gustavo shook his head, indicating he had no idea. Joey asked if Gustavo thought they may have heard them talking in the kitchen before slamming the rock against the door.

Gustavo's eyes opened wide. "Ah....that's why that box was stacked up against the house!"

"What box?"

"When I left the house to look for you, I saw a wooden crate leaning against the outside of the kitchen wall, just below the window. I had never seen the box before, but thought it may have just bounced off of a truck. They must have been standing on it listening to our conversation."

Joey was relieved. He could tell that Gustavo was surely telling the truth. Now, more than ever, Joey wanted to win. He wanted to defeat the thieves. But how would he get past the front door of the museum? They needed to hatch a plan.

13

Friendship

Joey and Gustavo started walking toward the museum. Joey had taken off the Bolivian poncho that Gustavo loaned him. He wanted the thieves to recognize him.

The boys walked all the way up *Calle Baptista* until they were standing across from the museum. The men immediately recognized them. All was going according to plan.

Joey held the gold headdress in his hand, gently tossing it in the air to be sure the men could see it.

"Want it? Come and get it," Joey called out to the men. "It's all yours."

The men looked at each other and smiled. They didn't understand much English, but they sensed they were close to getting the ancient headdress.

"Come on," Joey said. "Come get it." He held the headdress in his outstretched hand for both men to see.

The men crossed the street and strutted with confidence toward Joey, who was standing perfectly still with his arm extended toward the men. Gustavo started to slowly stroll down the street away from the men, who were focused entirely on Joey and the gold headdress clasped in his fingers.

"Is this what you want?" Joey asked, still holding the headdress in his hand.

The men came closer.

Joey waited until the men were almost close enough to touch the headdress, then he reached back and threw it over their heads.

"Ahhh," the men yelled. They looked skyward as they tracked the flight of the ancient artifact. Joey turned and ran the other way.

The men watched the headdress fly toward the museum, then noticed that someone was standing at the front door. It was Gustavo!

"Got it," he yelled, as he caught the perfect pass from Joey. He opened the door to the museum and walked in.

"No, no, no, no," the men cried. They fell to their knees and pounded the sidewalk. There was nothing they could do now. Joey was out of their sight and the headdress was safely inside the museum, where a guard was stationed at the front desk at all times.

Gustavo quickly told the guard about the men from the Quizquiz gang before rushing back to see the curator, the person whose job it is to make sure treasures like the headdress were kept safe. Gustavo had been in to see the curator before with his father, so he had no trouble finding her office. Meanwhile, the guard had called the police, who arrived quickly in their cars with flashing lights to arrest the two members of the Quizquiz gang.

After Gustavo left the headdress with the curator, who was elated to have such a priceless item in the safety of the museum, he met Joey at the lake as planned.

"Great plan," Gustavo said enthusiastically, giving Joey a high-five. Gustavo knew his father would be proud.

"Thanks," smiled Joey. "Nice catch."

"Nice catch? Nice pass!" Gustavo said back.

Joey could hardly believe that he had thrown such a perfect pass. This was definitely harder than any basketball game he had ever been in. As the boys walked along the lakeside toward Gustavo's house, Joey couldn't help but think about the next time his coach asked him if he wanted to go in the game. He wouldn't hesitate to say yes.

14

The Celebration

When the boys reached Gusatvo's house, they were surprised to see his father waiting on the front step.

"*Auqui!*" Gustavo shrieked. He was overjoyed to see that his father had come home from the hospital. He ran to his father and hugged him tight for a long time before introducing him to Joey.

"You boys are heroes," his father said, speaking in English so that Joey could understand.

"But...how do you...?" Gustavo wondered aloud.

"The museum called just as I arrived home. You were both very brave." The smile on his face revealed to the boys how proud he was of them.

"How about a celebration at our favorite restaurant?" Both of the boys smiled wide. They were definitely hungry.

"How about La Cupola?" Gustavo suggested. "It's my favorite place. You'll love it, I promise," he told Joey.

It was a short walk through the narrow Bolivian streets to get there. Joey couldn't read the menu, so he just ordered what

Gustavo and his father did: grilled trout caught fresh from Lake Titicaca. It was the reason Gustavo and his father loved the restaurant so much, and Joey agreed. He'd never had trout before, but couldn't believe how good it tasted. It was flaky and full of butter. As they ate, Gustavo's father told Joey all about the history of the Isla del Sol, which they could see clearly from their table. Joey was also surprised to learn that the other half of the lake was actually in Peru. The closest he'd been to Peru was Peru, Vermont, which named itself after the South American country many years ago in an effort to make itself more appealing to potential settlers. The real Peru seemed way cooler to Joey.

After their meal, the three walked back to the house. They made their way into Gustavo's room, which was the first time Joey began to think about his own room. He thought about his teepee and the mailbox on his desk that had started this whole adventure. He wondered if his family would be concerned that he was gone. Had they even noticed?

"So, how do I get home?" Joey asked.

Gustavo grinned. He remembered asking the same question after his first mailbox adventure in France. He fished through his desk looking for a piece of paper, then handed it to Joey.

"Write the word 'home' on this piece of paper and put it in the mailbox. It will take you back."

"That's it?" Joey asked.

"Yes, that's it. Would you like to go home now?"

"I think so."

Gustavo's father gave Joey a pencil from his pocket. "Thank you, Joey," Gustavo said quietly. "Without you, the headdress would have been lost to the Quizquiz gang."

Joey smiled as he looked up at his new friend. "I'm glad we got it to the museum safely. And I'm happy," Joey said looking at Gustavo's father, "that you are better Mr. Quispe."

"*Jisa*," they both said together. "We are happy too," Gustavo's father said as he gave his son a side hug.

"Maybe you can come to my house someday, in Vermont?"

Gustavo looked at his father, then nodded his head yes to Joey. "Send me a letter sometime. If you put my name on it, it will come straight to my mailbox."

Joey nodded as he folded the letter. He waved to Gustavo and his father, then dropped the piece of paper into the mailbox. With a quick burst of blue light and loud swoosh of air, he was gone.

15

Home Again

Joey was sitting again on his bedroom floor. He looked for the sapphire blue water of Lake Titicaca through the window but saw only green pine trees. He looked for the poncho that Gustavo had loaned him, but saw a pile of t-shirts instead. Then he saw his backpack. He glanced at his clock. It was still 12:24am.

Joey was confused. *It's the same time it was when I left,* he thought to himself. A sinking feeling came over Joey. *Was it all just a dream*?

He looked at the mailbox on his desk. It was not glowing. But he saw a piece of paper inside. Joey shuffled across the room, turned on the light, and reached into the mailbox. It was Gustavo's letter!

Joey was overjoyed. He grabbed the letter from the mailbox and put it under his mattress. He hoped that this letter would be the first in a collection of many. He crawled into his teepee, which is when he noticed that his pajamas were ripped. *They must have ripped when I dove to retrieve the map from the donkey's hoof,* Joey thought to himself.

He was tired, but he couldn't sleep. It had been an amazing night. Joey couldn't wait to tell Josie all about it, but he knew she wouldn't believe him, even if he did have the letter and ripped pajamas to prove it. The only way Josie would believe, Joey knew, is if she went on the next mailbox adventure with him.

Interesting Facts about Lake Titicaca

Lake Titicaca is one of the highest lakes in the world, at 12,500 feet above sea level. It is located in the Andes Mountains of South America, and because of the high altitude, is usually fairly cold. The average temperature at Lake Titicaca is 45 degrees Fahrenheit.

Because the lake sits on the border between Peru and Bolivia, you could get in your boat at Copacabana, Bolivia, and ride to Puno, Peru, in the same day!

There are over forty islands in Lake Titicaca. Isla Del Sol (Island of the Sun) is the most famous of the islands. It is where the people known as the Incas are believed to have first settled in the 15th Century. The Incas believe that the god of the sun was born on the Isla Del Sol. People lived on Isla Del Sol before the Incas, however. Archaeologists estimate that people first lived on the Isla Del Sol more than 3000 years before the Incas!

Most people in Bolivia and Peru speak Spanish. But many people who live on or near Lake Titicaca speak Quechua or

Aymara, which are ancient languages older than Spanish.

If you ever go to Lake Titicaca, you will also see several floating villages. These are made from a special type of reed, called totora, which grows in the lake. The Uros people, who lived on the lake before the Incas, first built these floating villages. Descendents of the Uros still build these floating villages today. Everything on the floating villages is made of totora reeds. The smaller villages have just a few round huts, for families to live in. Some of the larger islands also have a school, some stores, and a few even have a watchtower!

Hi Friends!

I hope you enjoyed the story about my first mail- box adventure. Bolivia is such an interesting place, and Lake Titicaca is the most beautiful lake I have ever seen!

Have you ever seen a beautiful lake? Have you ever received a letter from someone far away? I would love to read about it!

Here's my address:

Joey Jimmer-Jefferson
PO Box 867
Manchester, VT 05254

Be sure to include your return address. I will send a letter back! Happy writing!

Sincerely,

Joey

Made in United States
Troutdale, OR
06/05/2023

10450106R00038